Disaster at
LUNKER LAKE

BY DONALD G. KRAMER

Cover and Inside Illustrations: Dan Hatala

For information, contact
Perfection Learning® Corporation
1000 North Second Avenue, P.O. Box 500
Logan, Iowa 51546-0500
Phone: 800-831-4190 • Fax: 712-644-2392

Paperback ISBN 0-7891-5096-4
Cover Craft® ISBN 0-7807-9052-9

CONTENTS

1

READY FOR TAKEOFF

I kicked the push mower and wiped the sweat out of my eyes. Why did Dad have to spoil my summer vacation by telling me to mow the grass?

He stuck a list of stupid chores to the refrigerator door with this little fish magnet. Was that supposed to be some sort of joke?

I'd never have time to fish before school started if I did everything on his list! I'm only 15, I thought. I can't understand why I should have to work all the time.

"Better get to work, Tim," my little brother, Josh, called. He smirked at me as he went up the back stairs into the house. He was tossing his baseball and catching it again. Dad didn't give him chores to do.

I kicked the mower one last time and decided I'd had it. What a waste of an afternoon. If the grass got too deep, let Dad mow it. I was going on strike.

Ely. Ely, Minnesota. What a dumb name for a town. And what a dumb place to live. But Dad liked living here because he could give me lots of chores. He could make me shovel the snow in the winter and mow the grass in the summer.

When I'm 21, I'm going to move where I never see snow again, I thought. Or so much grass. Maybe I'll live in the desert. Let Josh mow the grass when I'm gone.

I headed toward the house to get something to drink. As I entered the kitchen, I saw Josh wandering into the family room. He had a bowl of ice cream in one hand and a video game in the other. *My* video game!

"Hey, Josh!" I yelled. "You'd better not be thinking about playing that game!"

"I'm not going to think about playing it," Josh answered. "I'm just going to do it!" He was smiling at me, daring me to do something about it.

That was it. I wasn't going to take it anymore. I had to slave away while Josh got to do whatever he wanted—including use *my* stuff! What a lazy bum, I thought. Even a sister would have been better than having him around!

I heard a knock on the door. I choked on a mouthful of cherry Kool-Aid as Josh plowed past me to answer it.

"Hi, Bob!" I heard him shout. Couldn't he keep it down to a dull roar? He was so obnoxious.

Bob, a family friend, came into the kitchen. He was wearing his uniform. But his shirt was untucked over his polyester pants.

Bob was a cop. I don't know why Ely needs cops, I thought. Nothing exciting ever happens here.

Bob tousled Josh's hair. Josh really looked up to Bob. Josh thought it would be cool to be a cop, I guess. But he's definitely too lazy for a job like that!

"Hi, boys," Bob said.

Josh answered Bob's greeting. And then he did it. He tossed my video game on the floor. On the floor! I had to paint Mrs. Henkel's whole garage and shed to make enough money to buy that game. It took me two days! And Josh thought he could do just whatever he wanted with it.

Well, I was going to let him have it. Although I couldn't really do what was going through my mind. After all, there was a cop in the house.

I was just getting ready to grab Josh by the hair when Bob interrupted me.

"Guys," he said, "I just got off work, and I'm dying to test out my new plane. How would you like to go with me?"

"New plane? That would be great!" I shouted, forgetting about injuring my brother for now.

One of Bob's hobbies was flying. He said it helped him relieve the stress of his job. How much stress could a cop have in Ely? I thought. Kids spray painting the Wolf Center on a dare is about all the crime we have.

"I'd love to try out your plane," I continued. "But, you know, Josh might get sick. We'd better not take him."

I did *not* want to take Josh. Partly because I knew once we got up in the sky, I would be too tempted to throw him out of the plane. *Without* a parachute!

Josh stuck his tongue out at me behind Bob's back. Then he crossed his eyes and pretended to barf on the floor. Real mature! Bob started to turn around. Then Josh looked all serious like he'd never been sick in his life.

"Tim is the one who threw up on the Octopus at the fair," Josh said. "Maybe *he* shouldn't fly with us."

I lunged for him. But Josh ducked out of the way and followed Bob, who was laughing. They were heading toward the living room. I sprinted after them. But I toned it down when I saw Mom. Bob explained the plan to her. She didn't look very sold on the idea.

"Come on, Mom," I begged. "But not Josh. He's a wuss."

"I know you are," Josh snapped. "Please, Mom? And let me take Fritz along."

I groaned and rolled my eyes. Fritz the mutt! Black and white with that long, ugly tongue of his. It was always dripping and hanging out the side of his mouth. I sometimes called him *Ugly* to make Josh mad.

Actually, I kind of liked Fritz too. But I didn't want to let Josh know that.

Too bad Ann, my sort-of girlfriend, and Rich, my best friend, were both on vacation. Maybe I could've asked one of them to go along. Then my dumb 12-year-old brother would have had to stay home. Whoever heard of taking a dog along on a plane ride anyway?

Mom called Dad to ask if it was okay for us to go with Bob. Mom wasn't so sure about it. You know how moms are—worrying all the time. It's their job, I think. But Dad trusted Bob. And I think he was tired of us complaining that there was nothing fun to do. I was sure glad he had said yes.

We rode in Bob's big gray car. Josh was hoping we'd get to take a squad car. But Bob explained how this wasn't "official police business." As Josh yapped away, I began to daydream about flying.

I couldn't wait to get in that plane. Maybe Bob would let me hold the wheel. I could see it now. I'd take control of that plane and show it who was boss. Just wait until Rich heard! He'd be so jealous. He hadn't been in a plane for a few years. And Ann! She would agree to go out with me for sure if she knew I flew all by myself!

The lake came into view and became a big, blue, shiny piece of glass. Little ringlets formed where fish were catching bugs off the shiny surface of the lake. But those were its only flaws.

As we went around a final corner, I saw it. I had to catch my breath. It was beautiful! It looked a lot nicer than the planes some of my friends' parents flew. Its silver floats rested on the smooth surface of the lake. And its red and white shiny paint glistened from the reflection of the clear lake water.

"I didn't know your plane takes off from the water," I said to Bob. "How cool!"

Bob replied, "Oh, yes. I wouldn't be able to land on any of the lakes and fish if it didn't."

It seemed unbelievable that in a little while, Josh, the dog, and I would be flying in this beautiful red and white plane. Sure beats mowing the lawn and playing ball with my stupid brother, I thought.

As we climbed into the plane, I noticed that the instrument panel was full of dials. It all looked foreign to me. For a moment I felt a twinge of fear. It looked so complicated. But I quickly reassured myself. Bob knew what he was doing.

He checked the necessary instruments and gauges. He said he wanted to make certain the plane was ready for takeoff. See, Bob's extra-careful, I told myself. After all, he's a cop!

Bob started the motor and checked the gauges once more. The propeller went round and round and made a purring noise. The wind from the propeller made a million small ripples near the plane when Bob increased its speed. I couldn't keep my stomach from doing a flip-flop.

"Are you scared, Tim?" I heard from the backseat.

I could've really hurt Josh at that point. But instead, I ignored him. I decided not to let him ruin my day.

And what a day this was going to be!

2
A Change of Plans

I looked out the window of the plane. Large waves were being made by the silver floats of the plane as we gained speed for takeoff. This was my first plane ride. And for a few seconds, I wondered why I had begged Mom to let me go.

I sure hope Josh gets sick in the backseat, I thought. That would serve him right. Although *my* stomach felt like I had eaten something really spoiled for lunch.

One second we were speeding across the water. And the next second we were hundreds of feet in the air. I felt like I had left my stomach down on the water.

I heard Josh laugh in the backseat. Maybe the plane ride felt different back there.

As Bob circled, I thought we were going to tip. I hung on to the seat as hard as I could. Once more I heard my stupid brother laugh.

Bob laughed, too, and said, "We'll be over your house in a minute."

I looked down to see what our house looked like from the air. I exclaimed, "Look at Mom hanging up clothes on the clothesline. She looks like an ant!"

The whole town of Ely looked so different from the air. I could see the Wolf Center and the college. And even Rich's house. They reminded me of the little buildings in the model train sets I used to set up.

"Hey, Bob!" I yelled. "There's where Dad works. I wonder if he can hear the plane?"

The motor continued making a purring noise. And the silver propeller was going around so fast it was only a blur on the front of the plane.

Then I decided to ask Bob the question that had been parading in my head ever since he had offered the plane ride. "Can we fly into Canada?" I asked. It seemed that everyone in Ely had been to Canada but me. Plus it would give me an even better story to tell Rich and Ann.

"Well, Tim, I didn't make my flight plans to include that sort of trip," Bob replied. "I don't know. We really shouldn't."

Bob looked over at me. I tried to act cool about it. But Bob could read the disappointment on my face. And he was the type of guy who never liked to let anyone down.

"But we need to get clearance anyway," Bob continued. "I haven't done that yet. So I'll radio the Ely airport to get clearance. Then I'll include the flight into Canada on the flight plan. We have plenty of gas and a new plane. Are you guys up for a short trip over Canada?"

"Yes!" Josh and I yelled. Fritz even barked in agreement.

After a few minutes of flying, I couldn't contain my excitement.

"This is awesome!" I said to Bob. "Thanks for thinking of us."

"I'm glad you're enjoying the flight," said Bob. "I

wish the radio weren't so full of static, though. I can't get the Ely airport to answer. I'll try again to announce our decision to fly over Canada."

Once more Bob tried to contact the Ely airport. But the radio continued to crackle with static. I could see that Bob was worried. And he kept shaking his left hand like it was asleep. I hate it when that happens!

I got a knot in my stomach when I noticed Bob's concern. But, I thought, what can go wrong anyway? Bob is a good pilot, and we have a new plane. Plus, he's a cop! I'll bet Dad will want to go next time.

Suddenly Bob's face lit up. A large smile appeared on his face. "I know where I'll take you guys!" he exclaimed. "My favorite fishing spot in Canada. It's a beautiful lake, and I've flown there many times. I call it 'Lunker Lake' because I've caught some really big fish there! Maybe we can do a little fishing before we go back."

We rode for a while in silence. I began daydreaming again. This time it was about Canada and Lunker Lake.

I couldn't wait to go fishing there. It seemed like once you fished in Canada, you had made it. You were big-time. You were ready for your own Saturday-morning fishing show.

I was planning the transcript of my first episode when the plane circled. Looking at Bob, I could see the smile on his face again.

But I saw something else too. I couldn't quite put my finger on it. It was sort of like a faraway look.

A shudder went through me as I realized what kind of look it was. It was the same look Dad had worn just before we slid on the ice last winter and skidded into the ditch. The look of terror.

But I looked at Bob again, and he seemed fine. I must've just read his face wrong, I thought. What could he be scared about anyway?

"What a cool-looking lake down there! Is this your Lunker Lake?" I asked Bob.

He smiled. "Yep, this is it," he said. "We'll circle and come down near the shore. Can you believe we are probably at least a hundred miles from any human being?"

Bob began making the landing approach on his Lunker Lake. I looked out the window and pictured myself reeling in a whopper.

What a day it was turning out to be. Two hours ago I had thought my life would waste away while I mowed and did all of Dad's other stupid chores. And now I was going to get to fish after all. And in Canada of all places!

All of a sudden my view became blurry. The plane had abruptly wobbled.

I turned quickly toward Bob. He was grabbing at his chest with one hand. What was wrong? I thought. It all seemed like I was watching it in a movie. We were going down . . . down . . . down.

After nearly touching the lake with the plane's floats, Bob made the plane climb once again. We barely missed a big pine tree with the right wing as we climbed skyward.

Now I was really scared. "What's wrong?!" I called out to Bob.

But Bob didn't reply. I looked over at him again. And I could see spittle dripping from his mouth. He let out a loud groan.

We made a wobbly turn. Once again Bob approached the water to land.

I knew Bob was sick. My mind began racing. *We are going to crash. We are going to die.*

It seemed that sheer willpower kept Bob conscious. We bumped into the water. My head flew forward. Water splashed up over the plane as we skimmed across the lake.

A loud groan once again escaped Bob's lips as we continued to travel fast on the water. I closed my eyes. But I opened them in time to see Bob, wincing in pain, cut the throttle to stop the engine.

But the plane continued on toward shore.

Branches screeched on the outside of the plane. It sounded like fingernails scratching a chalkboard. Only ten times louder.

A sudden bump threw Josh forward and against my seat. It threw me once again toward the windshield of the plane. We crashed through overhanging branches and brush. Finally the plane wedged itself against the shore.

Behind me, Josh was screaming. Fritz was barking. I could hear a strange high-pitched sound that seemed to be coming from me. I clenched my teeth on it.

Bob was the only one who wasn't making any noise.

I was staring straight ahead. I was in a daze.

"Bob," I tried to shout. But my voice was too thin. He couldn't hear me.

I took a deep breath and tried again. "Bob!" I shouted. "What's wrong?"

Maybe Josh and Fritz were making so much noise I couldn't hear Bob answer. I made myself turn and look at him. Then my stomach clenched.

His face was a strange color. He sat slumped over in his seat. The only thing that held him upright was the seat belt. His eyes remained open and glazed.

"Bob?" I called again.

Forcing my stomach down, I reached over to him.

19

I'd had first aid training with the Boy Scouts. I knew what to do as I felt for the pulse on his neck. When we'd received our merit badges, I'd taken Rich's pulse. And I could feel it right away. Now I couldn't feel anything!

I wished Bob's eyes were closed.

"Why did we crash, Tim? What's wrong with Bob?" Josh shouted at me.

I didn't know what to say. I didn't know how to tell Josh that our friend was dead.

Josh, Fritz, and I were stranded at Lunker Lake. We were possibly the only human beings for a hundred miles or more. Bob had said these same words just before we were getting ready to land.

I'm sorry I didn't do the chores, I thought. I'm sorry, Dad. Oh, Dad—I wish you were here. What are we going to do?

3

A HUNDRED MILES

I just sat there. I thought if I closed my eyes, I could open them up and find out it was just a dream. A really bad dream. It seemed so unreal.

But Josh's cries and the barking of Fritz brought me back to reality. I was the oldest. I had to make the right decisions. And I was responsible for my brother.

"Are you hurt?" I asked Josh.

"No," he sobbed. "I don't think so. I'm just kind of sore."

I looked down at myself. I didn't notice any major injuries. I felt my head, which was throbbing. My fingers ran across a big goose egg. But I'd had many bumps like that before. I was sure it would bruise. But it would heal.

All of a sudden an image of Mom and Dad popped into my head. Mom and Dad! What would they think when we didn't return home? They would be so worried. Oh, please, send someone to find us, I thought.

And then I remembered. Bob had never gotten through to the Ely airport. No one knew about the change of our flight plan. The search parties would be looking for us near Lake Superior. They didn't know that we had turned north into Canada.

My brain couldn't take much more thinking. So I tore open the door of the plane. Then I climbed down on the badly damaged float.

I helped Josh into the front of the plane. And

then to the float. I grabbed Fritz. And after a struggle, I managed to get him to shore.

Fritz didn't seem to be hurt at all. It was lucky that Josh had insisted we belt him in too.

I couldn't look in the pilot's seat, though. Because I knew what I would see.

I sat Josh on an old pine stump. He was still pretty shook up. He wouldn't stop crying, and he kept calling for Mom.

Fritz tried to lick his face and acted as if nothing had happened. I hoped that would help Josh calm down.

My thoughts once again became jumbled. I couldn't decide what to do first. Suddenly I felt something glide down my cheeks. I wiped at my wet cheeks and realized I was crying too.

I had to find some way out of this dilemma for all of us.

Looking around, I could see that the plane was too far under the trees. It had become wedged there on shore. Almost hidden. It couldn't be observed by any search plane that might fly over anyway.

Cold chills ran up my spine. Our lives depended on my decisions from now on.

And the first decision I had to make was the hardest. We would have to walk back to civilization. Wherever that was. We had no choice. I shared this decision with Josh.

"Walk?" Josh complained. "How far is that? Are you crazy? I don't want to walk that far. Why do we have to follow your stupid decisions anyway?"

I felt hot anger boiling inside me. I almost let my words explode from me. But then I quickly clamped my mouth shut, blocking their escape.

I decided not to answer Josh. I knew he was just scared. And he was expressing it by lashing out at me. It wouldn't do any good to get into a fight.

I've got to get Josh involved, I thought. Make him feel like he's part of the situation we're in. Get him to help with any ideas I think of. I've got to overlook his snot-nosed, annoying comments and get him to work with me.

With that thought in mind, I told Josh, "I'm going to the plane. I'll try to find anything I can for us to eat. Also something for us to sleep on tonight. Tomorrow we'll try to salvage everything useful that we can from the plane. I hope we can find some maps. We have to get ready for our long walk."

Josh followed me to the plane. As I opened the passenger door, I tried not to look at Bob. But I couldn't help it.

Tears once again welled up in my eyes. Why did

this have to happen? I thought. What started out to be a fun adventure has turned into the worst nightmare possible.

The cold, unmoving corpse continued to haunt my thoughts. I got the chills every time I got near Bob's seat.

Josh called up from where he was standing on the float of the plane. "Tim, do you think Bob had a heart attack?"

A heart attack. That must be it, I thought. Until this point I hadn't even given any thought to what had actually happened to Bob. I was so focused on us.

"I was sitting right there beside him," I replied as I painfully remembered. "I'm sure that's probably what happened."

I thought about what Bob had said about flying to relieve stress. I wondered if it was the stress that had caused his heart to go bad.

"You know, Josh," I continued. "We're lucky to be alive. We could've crashed and been hurt or killed. Bob made a huge effort to land the plane before he died." I got a lump in my throat as I thought about what could've happened.

My heart pounded, and I had a sick feeling in my stomach. But I knew the necessity of finding food and something to keep us warm.

I didn't know what I was looking for. So I just began searching. I looked under one of the backseats. And there, I found a new blue tarp. I almost jumped up and down with joy!

I shouted out to Josh what I had found. This tarp could be the thing to keep us warm and dry, I told him.

Josh stood on the bent silver float. And to my surprise, he was a willing helper.

I handed the tarp to Josh. I handed him other things as I found them. I found a roll of clothesline, two bags of popcorn, a container of sandwiches, and some apples and cookies.

The items Josh had piled on shore made me feel we now had a chance of surviving. I hoped we would find more when I searched the plane again tomorrow.

With a sense of dread and fear, I thought about the days ahead of us. I knew we faced a big challenge. And a brother who might not cooperate all the time didn't make things any easier.

Tonight will be the first challenge, I thought. We had to figure out where to sleep.

"Josh, I think the best place to sleep would be in the plane," I said. "It will be dry. And it will be easier to keep animals away from us."

Josh immediately stiffened. "I am not sleeping in there," he said. For once, he wasn't loud. He didn't yell. But the soft way he said it made him seem even more determined.

"I think it will be safer," I said. But I knew why Josh felt that way. And really, I felt the same. We did not want to sleep on the plane.

Not with Bob's corpse in the front seat.

The big red sun was resting on the horizon as it gave off its last light and warmth of the day. Then it would slowly disappear from the face of our part of the planet. Our first night in the Canadian wilderness was about to begin.

I told Josh, "We have to remember which way the sun is going down. If it's cloudy when we start to walk, we have to know for sure which way is west. Especially if we're lucky enough to find a map.

"See that dead tree?" I continued. "The sun is setting directly behind it. That will be our marker for west. Can you remember where you're standing now?"

"I'll remember," Josh answered. "Do you think we'll be able to sleep out here in the woods? I'm really tired."

"We'll have to try," I answered. I decided not to push anymore about sleeping in the plane.

Tomorrow, I realized, I would have to give the plane a complete search. We would have to carry anything we could use to help us make the trip back to civilization a reality.

Our meager supper consisted of three cookies, popcorn, and one sandwich each. We had three sandwiches. But Fritz had to eat too. I had my jackknife in my pocket. So I cut one of the apples in half.

Josh didn't want to eat his half. But I insisted. I knew future meals would not be as easy to find as this one.

As it started to get dark, shadows had a frightening effect on the landscape. I could visualize bears, ghosts, or anything at all if I let my imagination take control.

Josh started to cry. "I wish Mom or Dad were here," he whimpered. He huddled with Fritz, talking to him as if he were another human being.

The cool night breeze came drifting in off the lake. It wasn't completely dark yet. But it was beginning to cool off. I knew we would need a cover.

I took one end of the tarp, and Josh took the other. We laid it on the ground. We decided to lie on one half and cover ourselves with the other half. We'd have to figure out how to carry the tarp when we headed back toward civilization.

I couldn't believe I was thinking this. But I sure was glad my brother was here with me. Of course, it would've been better if I were stranded with

Rich or maybe Ann. But Josh wasn't so bad. At least I wasn't alone.

Once more I could almost hear Bob say, "Can you believe we are probably at least a hundred miles from any human being?"

Strange sounds continued to come from the forest around us. Fish jumped in the lake. They made strange splashing sounds. And the vision of Bob slumped over in the front seat of the plane kept floating before my eyes. Finally I dropped off into a restless sleep.

4
gearing up

Sometime during the early morning hours, the sound of tearing paper awakened me. Fear came upon me in a flash.

I couldn't remember where I was or what I was doing there. I woke up so confused. Like I was in a fog. Then I remembered. *Plane . . . Canada . . . Heart attack . . . Stranded . . .*

And now I heard a noise. I pulled myself farther under the tarp. I was hoping whatever was making the noise would go away. What if it was a bear or wolf? But once again I reminded myself that I was in charge.

I didn't want to look. But I forced my head out from under the tarp. I looked in the direction of the noise. With a sigh of relief, I saw three raccoon making short work of the popcorn. We had carelessly left it on the ground. Any animal could easily get at it.

Fritz had been sleeping on top of the foot of the tarp. Either he heard the noise. Or he smelled the coon while they were robbing us of our precious popcorn. Either way, he suddenly sprang up and chased those coon from our campsite.

It should've been common sense. *Don't leave food on the ground.* But my mind wasn't working correctly yet. I would have to be more careful, I thought.

I wasn't back to sleep long when I awoke to the light of the sunrise. The second day was about to begin. What to do? Which way to go? What to pack and what to leave? I knew I would have to make these decisions before the day was over.

Dew sparkled on the grass. And the sun was creating a red glare on the water as I looked toward the lake. It really was pretty. Everything looked fresh and clean.

All of a sudden I saw something peeking through the trees. Something that erased all the beauty and freshness. Something that seemed to taunt me with images of horror and decay.

I shuddered as I realized it was the nose of the plane. It was still at the edge of the lake. So was Bob, I thought.

I turned away. It seemed to burn my eyes to look that way any longer. So much that they were watering.

I decided I needed to wake up Josh. "Josh, time to get up!" I said.

I tried to sound cheerful. But inside, my stomach was full of all those Boy Scout knots I had learned to tie.

I knew I would have to face that plane again today. And the thought of entering it again almost made me sick. But I had to do it. I knew what I might find on the plane could mean life or death for my brother and me.

For breakfast, we, Fritz included, ate the last three cookies. The raccoon had been unable to eat those, thanks to the sealed container Bob had packed them in.

After eating, both Josh and I were overcome with thirst. Bob didn't leave any drinks in the plane. I looked around. Again, we had no choice. We had to dip water from the lake to drink.

"There's no way I'm drinking lake water!" Josh said. "That's sick!"

I wasn't finding the idea too appetizing either. But I knew that if we didn't drink anything, we'd become dehydrated. Then we'd really be in trouble.

"Fine," I told Josh. "Don't drink any. But I'm not going to pick you up and carry you when you've shriveled up like those dried apricots Mom buys."

I went to the lake and cupped my hands. I looked into the water. Big mistake. It was kind of murky. But I could see all kinds of creatures swimming around. I had to close my eyes. I was so thirsty, I managed to get some of the water down.

After I started drinking, I couldn't stop. It felt so good to wet my mouth. Pretty soon Josh did the same.

After we had drunk our fill of water, Josh looked at me and asked, "What are we going to do next?"

"Today we have to salvage anything useful in the plane," I replied. "We've found some things. Let's hope there are more survival supplies there."

When we got to the plane, I had Josh stand on the float once again. I said to him, "Just put the things I hand you in a pile. We'll sort out the useful stuff later."

I didn't want Josh to have to see Bob again.

I wiped my eyes. Funny how your eyes water when you feel scared sometimes, I thought.

My foot felt heavy as I raised it to get on the float beside Josh. I opened the passenger door and crawled to the backseats. I decided to start there.

I saw a dark brown, locked, wooden chest behind the backseats. Maybe it held some things we needed, I thought.

If I could've gotten the chest out of the plane, I might have been able to break into it with a big rock. But the chest was too big and heavy. So with much hesitation, I looked over the front seats. The keys were hanging in the ignition. I saw a smaller key than the rest on the ring. This had to be the one to the lock.

My eyes also couldn't help seeing Bob's gray corpse in the pilot seat. I almost lost my grip on the front seat. But I knew I had to retrieve those keys.

I took a deep breath. I reached over the seat. I had my eyes partly closed as I grabbed for the keys.

Just then I felt something scratchy. I quickly opened my eyes wide and realized that I had brushed Bob's polyester pants with my hand. His right leg felt stiff under the clothing. I couldn't get my air. And I felt sick and was trembling all over.

I panicked. I had to get out of the plane fast! But I knew I needed those keys. So with one last, fast grab, I retrieved them.

Just as I thought. The small key worked. I opened the brown chest. Looking at the contents, I realized that Bob had provided well for most emergencies. But, I wondered, would it be good enough for two boys and countless days in the wilderness?

I handed the items from the chest to Josh. I found two pencils and a notebook, an old blue cap, a hunting knife, a partial book of matches, a canteen, and a bright red backpack. I knew the backpack would come in handy.

I also found one other very important item. It was a collapsible fishing rod and four lures in a tube-type case. A sealed box of crackers was the last of the treasures from the chest. Those would be put to use immediately!

"I haven't found a map of Canada yet," I told Josh. "Let's hope it's in the storage compartment on the dash of the plane—if Bob had a map."

I glanced at Bob. His eyes remained open and glazed. His mouth was open as if he were gasping for one last breath before he died.

I felt like I was underwater. I couldn't get my

breath. And I felt as if I were sinking deeper and deeper into an abyss. Falling . . . falling . . . gasping for air.

"Tim!" I heard. But it sounded muffled and bubbly. Like when Josh and I used to try to scream after diving into the pool.

With a shudder, I opened my eyes. And I realized I had almost fainted.

But then I forced myself to look at Bob again. As I was closing my eyes before, something shiny near his waist had caught my eye. Was it . . .

I looked a little closer. Yes, it was Bob's gun. Since he had come to our house from work, his gun was still nestled in the holster around his waist.

I had never fired a gun. And frankly, I never wanted to. Guns kind of scared me.

Then I thought about what might await us in the wilderness. What if we ran into wild animals? A little hunting knife wasn't going to be much protection. And I had to think of my little brother. As much as he annoyed me, I knew deep down I'd want to protect him in any way I could. Even though he was a pain, he *was* my brother.

How would I get the gun, though? It was hanging on Bob's left hip. And I would need the shells that were in the holster too. I didn't really want to carry it in my hand. If I carried the gun in the backpack, I wouldn't be able to get to it quickly in the case of an emergency.

I had to get the holster.

I climbed out of the plane. And I went around to the pilot's door. The window was broken out. I stuck my arm in.

I held my breath. You can do it, I told myself. I focused my eyes on the holster and not on Bob's frozen face. I grabbed the holster delicately, careful not to touch Bob in the process. The buckle must be in the back, I thought. So I turned the holster. Turned . . . turned . . . turned . . . until finally I saw the buckle.

I reached a little farther over Bob's body to reach the buckle. With trembling hands, I unfastened it. Then I grabbed the holster and pulled it toward me. After it was over, I started to feel nauseated. I turned my head to the right and threw up.

I wanted to get as far away from the plane as possible. Then I remembered. I needed to look for maps.

I stepped over the mess I'd just made on the float. I still felt weak, and I was afraid I was about to be sick again.

I decided to go around to the passenger door again. I opened it wide and reached in. I quickly opened the storage compartment. Yes! Bob had put a large folded map of Canada and one of Minnesota in there. I quickly grabbed both maps.

"Look, Josh," I said as I jumped to the ground. I was trying to sound more excited than I was feeling. For Josh's sake. "A map of Canada. And one of Minnesota! Now we can decide which route to take!"

Josh answered with a glum, "I suppose." I could tell he wasn't looking forward to the long walk. It would be no nature hike, that's for sure.

The sun wasn't quite straight overhead. So I estimated the time to be about 11:00. I didn't have a watch. I remembered Bob had been wearing one. But I would have to take it off his wrist.

And I could not bring myself to go back into the plane again. After the holster incident, I knew I would not be able to make myself get that watch.

5

TicKS aND BeRRieS

Josh spread out the Canadian map. How lucky for us! Bob had circled his "Lunker Lake." Next, I spread out the map of Minnesota. I quickly spotted Ely. Just south of the Canadian border. Nestled in the middle of lakes with names like Burntside, Bald Eagle, and Birch. *Home.* Would I ever get home? I wondered.

I arranged the maps so we could see the flight route we had taken to Lunker Lake. The map showed a very large Canadian lake between us and Minnesota.

Josh slowly realized our difficulty. "There is no town even close to where we are," he said. "How are we going to know which way to go? How are we going to get home?"

Tears welled up in his eyes. He fell back and covered them. He said, "I wish I was home. I miss Mom and Dad."

I felt myself beginning to cry too. But I talked myself out of it. I had to stay focused if we were to see Ely again.

I decided that we should travel northwest. Farther into Canada. The decision was not an easy one. But we would have fewer large lakes to go around. I also decided we should try to reach the closest town. It appeared to be about 120 miles away.

I explained all of this to Josh. I only hoped he would cooperate in the days or weeks ahead.

After a few minutes I managed to get Josh settled down. He began handing me the items we had salvaged from the plane. I divided these items into piles.

The backpack was a valuable find. I would be carrying the largest load. So I put the backpack on my pile. I put the hunting knife on Josh's pile. I thought it would make him feel important.

I felt the holster around my waist. I had been wearing it for about an hour now. It felt heavy but reassuring.

The matches, all 20 of them, went into a small compartment on the backpack. The roomy backpack held many of the things we needed to take.

"I'm going to let you carry the tarp," I told Josh. "We'll need it for tonight. I think we can run pieces of clothesline through these holes," I said, pointing at the holes along the edge that were lined with brass eyelets. We can make a comfortable backpack-type bundle for you to carry. We'll try it tomorrow morning."

I decided we should wait until morning to start traveling. So we spent the afternoon resting up. A supper of an apple and dry crackers washed down with lake water was not the ideal meal for Josh. Or me. We can't survive on this, I thought. My stomach felt like it was ripping open. I thought about how easily I could get my hands on a cheeseburger with the works and french fries if we were home. We definitely needed something with more substance to get through this.

I realized I would have to catch fish. So I got the

fishing equipment ready for carrying. I now understood how important it would be to us.

It would soon be dark, I realized. The plane and Bob were already in the shadows.

The next morning I awoke after a restless sleep. I called out, "Wake up, Josh!"

The sun was coming up. And we had to make final preparations. We needed to make as many miles as we could the first day.

Josh and I folded the tarp as we had planned. We tied lengths of clothesline through the brass-ringed holes. Josh tried it on.

I immediately heard, "It's too heavy. I'm not going to carry this thing all day!"

Instead of getting angry, I tried to be patient with my little brother. But it was hard. "Okay. Try the backpack instead," I replied.

The backpack was three times as heavy. So it didn't take Josh long to realize that the tarp wouldn't be that bad.

I paced around the camp. I wanted to make sure we had everything we needed. Then I went out to the lake and took one last look at the plane.

I said a silent good-bye to Bob. At least we were leaving him in an area we could find on the map.

In a sense we knew where we were. It seemed like a baby's security blanket.

"Maybe we should stay another day," Josh said. I could tell he was scared. He had snuck up behind me. He was staring at the plane too.

Staying another day was very tempting. But I knew we couldn't afford to waste any more time. "It would only be one more day before we would get back home. We have to get started," I answered.

We packed up completely. And after one more complaint from Josh about how heavy the tarp was, we were on our way into the unknown.

However, we got off to a bad start. About an hour into our walk, we found ourselves in a type of brush that I had never seen before. It had long thorns. They slashed across our arms and legs as we walked. I carried Fritz to help him through.

Josh was grumbling about the thorns as we walked. But all of a sudden he stopped. For a moment he was silent. But then he let out a yell that probably could've been heard all the way back in Ely.

"Aaaaahhhh! Help!!" he screamed.

I looked at Josh and realized he was covered with little black bugs. Then I looked closer. Wood ticks!

Josh had always hated any type of bug. So when he saw several ticks crawling on him, he panicked.

He threw off everything he was carrying and undressed himself.

"Get them off my back! I can feel them crawling all over me!" he shouted.

Meanwhile, I began feeling as if I were full of wood ticks too! I threw off my pack and the fishing rod I was carrying. I had put it over my shoulder by tying a piece of clothesline toward both ends of the carrying case. Then I rushed to get my clothes off.

We picked almost two dozen of the hateful ticks off each other. We searched our clothes and everything we were carrying and found many more. I knew we would itch for the rest of the day.

After the episode with the ticks, we made good progress. Except that Josh scowled even more than usual. And he kept jumping and brushing at his skin.

It was important to get started in the correct direction we wanted to travel. Sometimes a swamp or brush made us change our direction for a short time. But we would correct it as soon as possible.

I had been taught in Boy Scouts about the danger of getting off track. One degree of error in direction at the beginning of a ten-mile hike becomes a major error at the end. And we had many miles to hike. We could miss an entire town or area we wanted to reach.

Josh was walking to my left. Suddenly he stopped

and pointed. "Look!" he cried. "Tim, here's a bunch of berries!"

We immediately unloaded our packs and stopped to eat berries and crackers. We didn't realize how hungry we were.

"You know, Tim, berries and crackers aren't so bad," Josh said. "Mom never fed us anything like this."

I smiled and replied, "If she would've, I'll bet we wouldn't have eaten it without complaining."

We had a good laugh when we looked at each other—even as tired as we were. It was the first laugh since the crash and the death of Bob. Our hands were stained from the berries. And we each wore a reddish black ring around our mouths. We looked kind of like clowns.

We kept eating until our stomachs felt somewhat full. We soon got all packed up again with everything we had been carrying. And we started in the direction we hoped to be the correct one.

I could tell Josh was getting tired. But I asked him if he could go a little farther.

"For a little while yet," he replied. "How long do you plan on walking?"

"We'll walk a ways more," I answered. "When we come to a lake, we'll set up camp. How'd you like fish for supper?"

Josh seemed to step a little higher. And his eyes shined brighter. He liked fish. But I wondered how he would like it roasted over an open fire without salt and pepper.

Soon it was Josh who yelled, "Tim! I see water through the trees ahead!"

We each did a little dance. We had survived the first day's hike!

I looked at the sun in the western sky. Then I told Josh, "Let's set up camp here for the night. I'll try to catch a few fish. We'll have a good supper. Why don't you try to find some berries?"

I walked toward the lake. And I noticed what Dad called "thunderheads" building up on the horizon of the western sky. It looked as if they were billowing a mile high. They looked like piles of cotton through the trees.

This was not a good sign. I hoped we wouldn't have a storm. But it certainly looked as if we would.

What would our third night out here in no-man's-land be like? I wondered.

6
WEATHERING THE STORM

Several casts with our fishing pole and I had my first crappie. I then cast near a leafy bunch of brush near shore. All of a sudden a huge fish struck my lure!

I only hoped to get this prize fish in and onto shore. This time I wasn't fishing for fun. This was supper!

The fish propelled itself into the air. I called for Josh but didn't get any response. Holy cow, this fish must weigh at least 20 pounds! I thought.

With a splash, the fish reentered the water. It took out some of the line that was left on the reel. I didn't want to break the line. And I couldn't risk losing the precious lure on the end of that line. Not to mention supper!

I reluctantly let the fish have its way. I had never seen a fish so big on the end of anyone's line. Once again it jumped into the air as if it wanted to fly.

The growling of my stomach kept me going. There was no way I was going to let that fish beat me and get away. Sweat was running into my eyes, but I hardly noticed.

I struggled for what seemed like an eternity. Then finally I had the monster fish near shore. I decided to hold the pole in one hand and try to grab the fish through the gill with the other.

But that fish did not cooperate one bit! I slowly reached toward it. I had my hand several inches from its gill. Just then the snap of its jaws made me jump and almost let loose of the rod.

The fish managed to swim out of reach. But when

I reeled it in once more, it came along the shore more readily. With a fast sweep of my hand, I was able to get my fingers into its gill. Then I hauled my beauty onto shore. Supper at last!

It was the biggest northern pike I had ever seen! At least 30 inches long. And big, sharp teeth to go with its mean appearance.

I lay back and wiped the sweat out of my eyes. Wouldn't Bob have been proud of me! I wondered if he'd ever caught a lunker like this from his Lunker Lake. I tossed the crappie back into the lake.

I headed back toward camp. I saw Josh coming from the opposite direction carrying berries he had picked. He had them all in the old blue cap we had found in the plane. He now called it *his* cap and wore it all day. Fritz, as usual, was at his side.

"Tim, I found a lot of berries!" Josh called.

Holding the fish up, I called, "Look what I caught!"

I realized that to Josh, his berries were also an important find. He was as proud of providing part of our meal as I was.

"Great job, Josh!" I told him. "We'll have a good meal tonight." This brought a smile and a proud look to Josh's face. I realized a word of praise now and then would go a long way. It might keep Josh in a helpful mood.

"How did you ever get such a big fish to shore?" Josh asked. "He must be four feet long! Did he fight real hard? I bet he'll taste good. Am I ever hungry. How are we going to fry it?"

Lots of questions from an excited brother.

"Here's my plan," I replied. "We'll cut a couple of branches that look like a 'Y' off a nearby tree."

We did this. Then we cut a straight branch. Next, we sharpened one end.

Then it was time to clean the fish. Dad was always in charge of that. "How about it?" I asked Josh.

"That's okay," he replied. "You can do the honors." He handed me the hunting knife he was carrying.

After I killed the fish, I closed my eyes and tried to picture how Dad filleted fish. I had seen him do it many times. But I wished I had paid better attention.

First I turned the fish on its side with its backbone closest to me. Then I cut behind the gills until I hit the backbone. Josh turned away. Then I cut along the backbone to the tail.

"Do you remember what Dad does next?" I asked.

"I've never really watched," Josh replied.

What a help he was!

I thought I remembered Dad opening the fish. So I made a long incision. When I looked inside, I almost lost all of those berries I had eaten.

I knew I had to get the skin off. It was too tough to eat. So I slipped the knife between the meat and the skin and worked until I got it off. It took me a while. But I was proud of myself for doing so well for my first time.

Lastly, I slipped the knife in between the meat and the bones and removed the meat. Then I had to flip over the fish and do the same thing to the other side.

When I was finally finished, I was surprised at how much meat I got from one fish!

Next came the fire. I had been taught how to do this in the Boy Scouts. I tried hard to remember everything we'd learned. I had Josh gather some twigs, grass, and bark and tear bits of paper from the notebook.

Next we had to light the match. "Remember, we only have 20 matches. We can't waste any!" I warned Josh.

I had unsure fingers. And Josh was trying to shield the flame with his cupped hands. The match flamed. It turned orange. And then it went out. Nothing but smoke!

I stood up. I walked away from the area and wiped my eyes. Something was in them. What was wrong with me? I had almost let raccoon get our food. And now I couldn't even light a fire. How many more matches were we going to waste? And what would happen to us if I continued doing dumb things?

Josh looked at me. He didn't seem to understand what the big deal was.

"Josh, we wasted a match!" I said.

Josh said, "So what? Let's try again."

With less confidence, I did try again. This time the match flared a beautiful red flame. The dry grass smoked, and a tiny flame appeared.

I nursed the tiny flame with dry, small pieces of bark and dry grass. And then small twigs. We had a fire!

Soon larger branches were burning. We hung the fish over the crackling fire between the two "Y" pieces of wood. To me, getting the fire burning was a boost of confidence. We would have to do this many times before we were back to civilization.

I walked a short distance to the west to get a better look at the sky. The clouds were rolling.

"I'm afraid we're going to have a bad storm," I said to Josh. "We can let the fish roast and set up camp at the same time. We've got to think of another way to sleep, or we'll get wet."

"Let's make the tarp into a tent," Josh suggested.

"How?" I asked. Then the idea came to me. I saw two small trees about seven feet apart.

"Great idea!" I told Josh. "We'll tie the

clothesline between those two trees over there. We can tie it just high enough so we can crawl under it. Then we'll put one end of the tarp over it and sleep on the rest of it! If we're lucky, we might have a little of the tarp to cover ourselves with."

We tried it. And it worked even better than I thought it would! But would it be okay in a storm? I wondered.

Meanwhile, the fish was turning a tan color over the fire. A few spots near the fire were charcoal black.

We sat down on the ground and had our fish and berries. The fish actually tasted good! And Josh didn't even complain about not having salt or pepper.

After finishing our meal, we had a nice amount of roasted fish left. The next question was where to store the rest of it.

We decided to wrap the leftover fish in leaves and store it in our backpack. We took a chance and put it in the makeshift tent. We couldn't hang it in a tree in the rain. And we figured the rain would keep away the animals. We hoped, anyway.

In the distance, I heard the rumble of thunder. The rain began as a mist and soon turned into a rainstorm. Several little rivers of rainwater made their way across the tarp we lay on. But at least we had our so-called tarp tent. Still, how I wished we were home with a solid roof over our heads.

The wind began to howl. Suddenly the first bolt of lightning lit up the world around us! The thunder that followed shook the ground. Then it rumbled itself into silence.

Soon came another flash of lightning. Brighter than the first one. And a crash of thunder made us both jump out of our skin. Then we heard the sound of a falling tree or a large branch mingled with another loud thunder explosion.

Josh was quiet. Most likely he was too scared to talk. But with the next lightning flash, he sprang upright. When his head hit the top of the tent, he came back to reality. He sat as close to me as he could and didn't say a word. I could feel him tremble once in a while. I tried to comfort him. After all, he was just a kid.

Meanwhile, rain continued to pour. It made the drops on our tarp sound like a million people trying to play a drum. And we were inside of it.

We spent the next hours cuddled close together. Josh, Fritz, and me.

Finally, sometime toward morning, the storm moved on. We finally settled down to a well-deserved sleep.

Sunrise came too soon. The storm had left

fallen branches. But once again the sun was going to smile on us today. As the sun came up, it wore a dull orange color. It looked as if the rain had washed the color from its face.

Fog was coming from the lower areas and the swamp near us. The wilderness looked full of many smokestacks. Raindrops were clinging to the branches of the forest. They looked like millions of diamonds just waiting to be picked.

"I feel older than I did just a few days ago," Josh said as we got up and stretched. Then he paused.

"I wonder if Mom and Dad think we're dead," he said. "They'll be surprised when we get to a place where we can call them."

Once again we folded the tarp into a makeshift bundle for Josh to carry. I put on my backpack and picked up the fishing gear. We were ready to face the unknown again. On our way to where? We really didn't know. Just someplace out of this forest. Someplace with people.

7

fRitz TO THE RESCUE

The ground squished from the rain of the night before as we walked. Fog hung over the lakes. And the sun warmed the land. Up until now it hadn't been too hot. But I had a feeling that today would be different.

As we walked, I was deep in thought. Were we going in the right direction? I wondered.

"I've got to rest," Josh said after a little while. "My legs are killing me!"

I had to bite my tongue. This is not the time to be lazy, I wanted to say. We needed to keep moving. But Josh was younger. And he had been doing a good job of keeping up.

"Okay, we can rest for a while," I said.

I was tired, too, I realized. We both napped. Then we set off again. "Let's walk a ways more," I said. "Just until we find a lake."

We continued on our way. And sure enough, we finally did find a lake. By now it was getting close to suppertime.

"I didn't think I could make it," Josh said once we got there.

"Don't give up yet," I said. "I want you to find some berries to go with the fish I hope to catch. You should find some close to camp."

Once again after a little grumbling, Josh went berry-picking. And I went fishing.

I was thankful the fish were hungry. I caught ten sunfish. Their green color, orange bellies, and blue gills made them a beautiful fish.

But I decided on one cast too many. I cast out and didn't realize that I had cast over a tree or something that was in the water. My treasured lure was hooked. And I could not get it unhooked.

I only had two lures left. What if I lost those? I had to rescue this one. So I took off all my clothes and waded and swam to unhook the lure. Well, at least I got a bath, I thought.

I arrived back at camp before Josh. All the fish were cleaned when he finally returned. I was getting the hang of it now.

Once again Josh had a grin on his face. He presented me with his cap full of berries.

We lit the fire with only one match. Then we roasted the fish. Our supper consisted of berries and fish. The crackers were all gone.

Josh complained, "I hope we can find something instead of fish and berries pretty soon. I'm getting sick of them."

For the first time we were bothered by mosquitoes. It must've been the rain. They seemed to swarm over us, leaving welts on every exposed part of our bodies. What did Dad call them? Oh yes, I remembered. "The Minnesota state bird." But they had them in Canada too! I noticed that they stayed away from the fire. So Josh and I huddled there.

During the night I heard Fritz growl. I also heard something growl back from the nearby brush. What was it?

I dug deeper into the tarp and moved closer to

Josh. I heard the crack of a twig close to the tarp. To my relief, it was Fritz. He was making sure the animal was gone.

What had been spying on us? Was it afraid of humans? Or did it think of us as a meal?

I couldn't get back to sleep. I worried about the growl from the bush. And how many other problems awaited us? I wondered. Most of all, I hoped we were heading in the right direction.

The next morning I started keeping a logbook. I decided to start with a few notes on things that seemed important to remember. Or things that seemed unusual or interesting. I was certain many other things would happen in the days ahead.

I crawled as quietly as I could from under the tarp. I didn't want to wake Josh. I took the notebook and pencil out of the backpack. Then I walked to the lake. I sat on the ground and leaned back on an old pine tree.

Things to Remember:
-Keep fire burning.
-Don't leave food where animals can get it.
-Try to be patient with Josh.
-Keep going in one direction.

As I made a note about the plane and the death of Bob, I cringed. Funny, I thought, how four days after the crash, tears still formed in my eyes.

I smiled as I thought about how we'd come a long way already. We've done real well so far, I told myself. Mom and Dad would be proud.

My usual, "Time to get up, Josh," did not bring much response. Josh peeked out from under the tarp. And he informed me he wanted to sleep a little longer.

I wasn't happy with that answer. So I kept poking and prodding him until finally he crawled out. But I could see by the sullen look on his face that he would be in a bad mood.

"I wish we could have something else to eat once," Josh grumbled.

"We will. As soon as we get to a town, Josh," I assured him.

His reply was, "I wish we were at home. Mom's cooking would taste better than what you make." I just smiled. Mom would enjoy hearing that one after we got back home.

We soon were on our way into the unknown. Once more.

During the early part of the afternoon, we were passing a large clump of berry bushes. My thoughts were on the days ahead, planning what I'd be doing when I got home. Fritz was roaming somewhere in front of us. And Josh was following behind me.

I heard movement in the clump of berry bushes near me. But I didn't pay much attention. I just thought it was Fritz.

But what I saw come out of the bushes rooted me to the spot for a second. Then I called to Josh to run.

"It's a bear!" I screamed.

The black, heavy pistol I had been carrying on my belt every day became a sudden comfort. I tried to get the pistol free of the holster as I ran close behind Josh. Josh had thrown the blue tarp off his back so he could run faster.

For some reason, the bear stopped for a few seconds to sniff at the tarp. Those seconds made it possible for Josh and me to climb quickly into a couple of trees.

Then the big bear came lumbering toward us. It was black with brown on its muzzle. When it raised its nose in the air to sniff, I could see that it had a white patch below its throat. Josh and I were hanging on to branches. Josh was crying, and I was shaking with fear.

The bear continued to stretch and reach with its front paws. It was trying to reach Josh. He was trying to climb higher. But he was about as high as he could go.

We both were afraid of what would happen if it

got hold of one of us. And I knew it would only be a short time before it decided to try to climb one of the trees.

I had to do something. I had to save my brother. So I took the pistol the rest of the way out of the holster. Nervously, I plucked a bullet from its place in the belt.

My mind was racing, trying to figure out how to load the gun. When suddenly out of the brush came a blur of black and white. It was running toward the bear.

To my surprise, Fritz was coming to the rescue!

He made a pass at the bear. He was running and biting at its back legs. The bear got down on all four feet. It made an attempt to knock Fritz down with one of its front paws. And it grazed the dog's back.

But Fritz came back at the bear. I could see blood on Fritz's back. But this didn't stop him. He nipped the bear on one of its legs.

Time after time Fritz risked his life to save ours as he rushed at the bear and barked. It seemed as if the bear forgot we were in the trees above. With Fritz close behind, the bear finally retreated into the surrounding forest.

The sound of Josh screaming shattered my state of shock. We were both shaking as we climbed out of the trees.

Josh immediately hugged me. He was shaking. And so was I.

I knew that both of us had never been this frightened before.

"Where's Fritz?" Josh asked as we looked around. Fritz's blood lay on the ground making a small puddle. But Fritz was nowhere in sight.

Josh started to cry. "Fritz!" he yelled. "Come on, Fritz! Come back, boy!"

A feeling of sadness washed over me. That dog had saved our lives. And in doing this, he had possibly sacrificed his own.

I walked a few feet to where the tarp lay. Luckily, it wasn't damaged.

Suddenly I heard Josh scream again. This time, though, he was screaming, "Fritz! You came back!"

I ran toward Josh and Fritz, who had come hobbling back. He was even wagging his tail. Both Josh and I praised him and gave him hug after hug.

"I thought you were a goner," Josh said to Fritz.

But the claws of the bear had only grazed Fritz's back. They had made several shallow slashes. The blood made the wounds look more serious than they actually were. I poured some lake water from the canteen on Fritz's back to clean the cuts.

We then continued on our way. But we didn't walk quite as fast this time. Fritz needed to go a little slower. And we didn't want to wear him out.

We walked until the sun was settling below the horizon for the night. We didn't come to a lake this time. I had checked the map earlier in the day. And I was certain we were going to have a night without water or fish to eat.

So we picked berries for food. I had used the last of the water in the canteen for Fritz. So the juice from the berries was the only moisture we were going to have.

We made preparations for the fire. And we got it going with only one match.

"Sixteen matches left," I said to Josh.

For the first time since leaving the plane area, Josh and I heard the sound of a wolf pack in the distance. I knew I'd be up several times to keep the fire going tonight.

The nights were getting colder. Josh and I cuddled under the tarp. We lay close for warmth and a feeling of security. Josh was so tired that he immediately fell asleep.

My responsibilities kept me awake though. Thoughts of the new threat of wolves in the area made me nervous. And I worried about keeping the fire going during the night. And on top of it all, thoughts of Mom and Dad worrying about us kept me from a good night's sleep.

TWiSTS of fate

The next morning when I called Josh to get up, he was grumpy. When he did crawl out from under the tarp, he complained, "I'm hungry."

But there wasn't anything to eat. So we made

hasty preparations to get on our way. Fritz was roaming in the woods ahead. Josh was bringing up the rear. He was still grumbling that he was hungry. We had begun our fourth day of traveling away from Bob's Lunker Lake.

We were making good progress when Josh went down. He had stumbled on a root and twisted his ankle. He fell on a flat rock, landing on his knee. He tried to get up. But he let out a cry when he put any weight on his right foot.

"Tim, Tim! Help me," I heard. "I can't stand on my foot. And my knee is bleeding!"

In frustration, I took off my backpack. I threw it on the ground as hard as I could. Will anything ever go right? I said to myself.

As I ran over to Josh, I could see he was in pain. I didn't have any bandages. Or anything with which to wrap the ankle.

I made Josh lie down on the tarp. Then I tried to figure out where to get some bandage material. I decided to cut several inches off the bottom of my shirt. It would make a good wrapping for his ankle and a bandage for his knee.

Josh continued to squirm and sob. I told him his ankle would feel better after it was wrapped. At least I hoped it would. I could only hope the ankle wasn't broken.

After his ankle was wrapped, I wrapped his knee. This was only a bad scrape. But the ankle could pose a problem, I thought.

Josh asked me, "Are you sure my ankle isn't broke? It still hurts."

"I'm sure it's only sprained," I replied. But I wasn't really sure.

"We'll have to see how your ankle feels tomorrow morning," I said. "If you can't travel on it, we will have to stay another day."

Food. We needed food, I thought. And now Josh couldn't help.

I found a stone and put Josh's injured foot on it. A little elevation might keep the swelling down some, anyway.

"There should be a lake not too far from here," I told Josh. "I'm going to build a fire. Then I'll try to find the lake. I'll try to find us something to eat."

This time I needed three matches to get the fire going. Only 13 matches left. How many days left? I would have to be more careful and get really dry tinder when starting a fire. Too many problems today had made me careless.

I borrowed Josh's now dirty cap to bring back any berries I hoped to find. I took my fishing pole and canteen. And I headed northwest to find the lake that was noted on the map.

As I walked, my throat felt dry. And a cold feeling started between my shoulder blades. What if Josh's ankle was broken? I couldn't possibly leave him alone and walk to find help.

All the *ifs* caused tears to flow down my cheeks. And I angrily brushed them away. Had anyone been in a worse mess than we were in right now? I wondered.

This time I found a clump of red raspberries. First I stuffed my face. I needed energy to keep going. Then I filled Josh's cap with the rest of the ripest ones.

As I walked on, I soon saw the sun glinting off a lake that looked like a mile of glistening silver. I hoped this clear pool of water was full of fish— any kind of fish.

The fish bit on my lure like they were hungry too. In less than 15 minutes, I had ten beautiful crappies and a perch lying on the bank a safe distance from the water.

While I was casting, I noticed the mosquitoes. They were around my face. They kept trying to go up my nose. And I couldn't swat them away because I needed both hands to cast. They were biting more often than I had noticed before.

When I got back to camp, I noticed Josh was having more problems with the mosquitoes than I had experienced. He couldn't move around on his sprained ankle. And this made him prime bait. I moved him closer to the fire, hoping it would help.

I cleaned the fish. By now I was feeling like a pro at it. Wouldn't Dad be surprised? I thought. Then I put them over the fire to roast. We could hardly wait to eat. We were both so hungry that Josh didn't even complain about another meal of fish and berries.

We again moved the tarp as near the fire as I felt was safe. By sundown we were both under the tarp.

The smoke from the fire did keep the mosquitoes away. And by keeping the fire going all day, we had saved at least one match. I decided to keep the fire alive until we could move again. I hoped that would be soon!

I popped my head out from under the tarp at sunrise. A beautiful, blue cloudless sky awaited us. And a brilliant yellow sun shone. Now if only Josh's ankle would let us walk. We could at least make a few miles today.

I shook Josh to wake him. He opened his eyes. But he didn't seem to appreciate the disturbance of his sleep. He moved his injured ankle and winced. It looked like we would be at this campsite at least one more day.

"See if you think you'll be able to walk on your ankle," I told Josh. Maybe it was just stiff, I hoped.

He carefully crawled out from under the tarp. He stood up. But when he tried to take a step, he could only hobble.

"It's better, Tim," he said, "But I can't walk on it very good."

At least now I knew that Josh's ankle was only sprained and not broken. That was a big relief. Yet we would have to spend at least another day here at this spot.

So I had plenty of time to write in my logbook.

I'm trying hard to be brave. But it's hard. I know I have to be strong for my brother. He's counting on me. But I just wish I could count on someone else. It's hard being responsible for everything. Maybe that's what Dad was trying to teach me by making me do all those chores. Sounds so easy now compared to finding food and shelter and treating injuries . . . .

Around noon the sun was bright and generating heat. It was the warmest day since we had started walking.

"How about letting me wash all our stinking clothes?" I asked Josh. "It's warm enough that we won't get cold while I wash them and they dry."

I took all the clothes to the lake. I jumped into the cool water and began washing our clothes. As I was washing the socks, I noticed small holes beginning to show at the heels. We needed good, clean socks to prevent blisters. I'd have to watch for this when we started walking again. Maybe if the holes got too bad, we could find thick leaves to stick in the heels of our shoes.

As I was heading back toward shore, clothes in hand, I suddenly stepped on something. It seemed to slither underneath my feet. I screamed. I didn't mean to act like a baby, but I couldn't help it. Then I looked through the clear water and saw a long snake swimming away.

I yelled again. I hated snakes more than anything. I know guys are supposed to like things like snakes. But not me. I was so sick of being in the wilderness! I was sick of surprises! I just wanted to crawl into my safe bed at home and pull the covers over my head.

I took the clean clothes back to camp. I hung them on any branches I could find.

The clothes dried fast in the warm sun. We ate the remainder of the berries and the fish. I only hoped that Josh's ankle would permit us to travel tomorrow.

The next morning I woke up to another nice day. The sun was coming up a bright orange color. Some fog was rising from a swamp in the direction we were going to walk—if Josh's foot would allow it.

Josh crawled out from under the tarp.

"Do you think you will be able to walk on your sore ankle?" I asked.

He limped. But he said he would try to go as long as he could. "I think I should keep the wrapping on the ankle," he said.

"Even a few miles will help," I told him.

I carried the tarp in addition to my usual load. It was heavy. But I realized any extra weight would make it impossible for Josh to travel.

All of a sudden an unusual sound broke the silence of the forest. But it was a sound we had heard before. I couldn't place it at first. Then I realized . . .

It was a plane! It was flying low over the lake where I had caught the fish the day before.

I looked at Josh, and he looked at me. Our mouths hung open. It seemed so long since we'd heard this welcome sound.

Josh and I shouted as loud as we could! We jumped up and down. We waved our arms!

But the plane did not fly directly over us. And the pilot didn't make any sign that he had seen us.

"Do you think they were looking for us?" Josh asked. Tears were running down his cheeks.

"I doubt it," I said. I was getting angry now. It seemed that we would be stuck in the wilderness forever. "I bet it was someone like Bob. Just looking over his favorite lake in Canada. Why didn't he stop and fish? Why didn't he see us?"

My questions hung in the air.

We started walking again. What other choice did we have? But we didn't get very far when I heard Josh say, "I can't go much farther. My ankle is killing me!"

We rested a short while on an old log. And I looked over the Canadian map. It appeared as if we were on a path that went along a chain of lakes. One was connected to the other by a narrow band of water. The lake we were approaching appeared to be connected to the lake I had caught the fish in yesterday.

After a short rest we started walking once more. But we couldn't go very long until we had to stop for Josh's ankle again. But luckily we had made it to a lake.

The lake was a clear blue. Hardly a ripple was on its surface. A large fish jumped out of the water. It looked like a bass or a large crappie.

What kind would we have for supper tonight? I wondered.

It didn't take long before I had caught some large crappies and sunfish. When I got back to camp, Josh actually helped me clean the fish. Now Dad would *really* be surprised!

We had a few fish left and a small ration of berries. I didn't want them to draw animals to our camp. So I put the leftovers in the backpack. I found a tree to hang them in. I climbed the tree and began tying the backpack to a branch.

While I was tying, my left foot slipped. And I fell almost ten feet to the ground!

I lay on the ground, stunned and unable to take a breath. I had landed on my back and knocked the wind out of myself. Josh started to scream.

"Tim, are you hurt?" he cried.

I managed to croak out that I'd be okay. The big problem was that I couldn't get my air. I finally was able to get up. But I knew I'd be stiff tomorrow. Just one more problem, I thought.

I've got to be more careful, I scolded myself. What if I got hurt? Then we'd really be in trouble!

Once more I wished that when Bob had come over, we hadn't been home.

9

Rats, an Apple Tree, and an Angry Moose

Morning again. Our ninth day of being stranded in the wilderness. Boy, was I stiff from my fall. I was very lucky not to have broken a bone or two.

I took a slow walk to the lake. I wanted to stretch my aching muscles and bones before our long hike. I stared into the shiny surface of the lake. I saw shadows of the trees along the bank reflected on it. In any other situation, I would only see the beauty of this place, I thought. But now I couldn't help picturing the hidden dangers. They lurked in the placid lakes and behind the majestic trees.

I slowly returned to camp. Josh was still sleeping. So I wrote a few notes in the logbook.

I have to be more careful. My fall yesterday could've meant the end for Josh and me. After being in the wilderness for over a week, I'm kind of getting used to this place. But that's the bad part. I don't want to get used to it. I want to get home. I want to get Josh and Fritz home. I don't want there to be any more accidents or surprises. I want to finish mowing the lawn . . . .

When I was tired of writing, I called to Josh, "Josh, time to meet the sunrise! We've got to get on our way!"

Josh got up and stretched. Then he said, "Hey, Tim, my ankle feels better!"

Finally some welcome news.

We continued following a northwesterly direction. I carried everything again. Josh was still favoring his ankle.

As we were walking, I noticed something new.

I called to Josh, "Hey, Josh, look at this! It looks like an old logging road. And it goes in the direction we're going!"

"Maybe we can follow it," Josh said. "It would make walking easier."

"I think you're right," I said. "Maybe this trail will lead us to a town. Or at least a main road!"

We continued to follow the old trail. And up ahead we could see a huge, open area.

"This must be where the logging was done," I said. "This road was used for hauling the logs somewhere. But the brush that has grown up is quite a few years old."

"Look over there on the far side. I see some buildings!" Josh called out excitedly.

We both were excited. I figured we wouldn't find people. It looked deserted. But at least this was something different! We had grown tired of the same scenery of trees, lakes, and berry bushes.

We ran over to the buildings. We could see that they had not been used for at least ten years.

"Hey, Josh," I said. "We shouldn't tire your ankle

too much. Should we stay here for the night? Maybe we can use the old bunkhouse to sleep in. It's midafternoon anyway. There should be a lake nearby to catch some fish."

Josh agreed. He went to find some berries. Fritz went exploring. His back was healing. And he was back to his old, energetic self. I went fishing. We all were successful.

Fritz had a good time chasing mice. He even caught some for his supper.

I thought I had seen the sun shining on a lake to the west. I was right, and the fish were hungry.

Josh found a few more berries. Not as many as we had been used to gathering. But enough to make the fish a little more tasty.

We decided to eat our meal in the bunkhouse. I hung the fish to roast over the fire near the door of the bunkhouse.

We used the table the loggers had eaten on years before. We had tried to clean it as best as we could. Funny, but the meal even tasted better, I thought, when we sat at the table.

We decided to sleep in the bunkhouse. As darkness approached, we lay the tarp on the floor. Both of us were tired. It was so nice to have a roof over our heads. And we went right to sleep.

Sometime during the night, I heard a scream. It was Josh!

"Something is in the tarp!" I heard Josh exclaim. "It tried to crawl on me!" He jumped up. I could tell he was really frightened.

Moonlight was coming through the window. And I could see several hairy things on the floor.

Rats! We were trying to sleep in a building infested with rats!

"Let's get out of here!" I shouted. "We'll put the tarp outside. I'm not going to sleep in here!"

Our first night under a roof in a while was spoiled.

In the morning I let Josh sleep. I recorded my thoughts in the logbook.

I wonder who used to stay here. How long has the place been deserted? I hope we get to sleep under a roof again soon—one without rats!

The mice and rats were once again in hiding as it was light outside. I took a chance and walked inside the bunkhouse. The sun beamed in the window facing the east. The glass panes were gone.

When will we see the sun come up through a window again? Even if the rats caused us some problems, it was a change. I'm glad we found this place.

I've been thinking about what's important. Before, I thought that hanging out with my friends and having fun were the most important things in the world. I didn't understand why Mom and Dad made such a big deal about school and doing chores. Stuff like that. But now I'm beginning to understand. What's important is doing your part. Looking out for your family. Being responsible. I'm starting to feel bad that I've been giving them such a hard time lately. Especially since they probably think we're dead.

"Come on, Josh," I said. "We've got to be on our way. We lost a few hours of traveling time by staying here yesterday afternoon. But the rest was good for both of us."

I had hung the backpack on a low tree limb. I saw where some small teeth had tried to gnaw a hole in it. But luckily the creatures hadn't been successful.

We ate our cold fish and began our walk northwest. The old trail continued to be on our planned route.

We were close to another small lake. I was daydreaming again. Not much else to do when you walk. Especially when everything looks the same—day after day.

All of a sudden a giant splash and strange noise brought me back to the present. A huge moose had come out of the water. It had a very large set of antlers and a dirty, brown shaggy coat.

The moose looked mean as it shook the water off itself. And it was staring at us. It pawed at the ground and acted as if it were king and we were in its kingdom.

Josh let out a scream, "I can't run! My foot still hurts! Help me, Tim!"

"Wait a minute," I said. I remembered watching a Canadian wildlife show on TV that featured moose. Even though they were huge and looked menacing, I remembered that they don't usually attack humans.

"Just stand here and be quiet," I told Josh. He stood beside me, trembling and sniffling. Suddenly the moose stretched its neck forward and gave off an angry bellow.

Josh and I both were rooted to the spot where we stood. It was still watching us. But it quickly got bored with us. It became concerned instead with the swarm of flies that seemed to be invading its dark brown coat.

"See, Josh?" I said. "It's nothing to be afraid of." Josh looked at me and smiled.

But a black-and-white blur broke our moment communing with nature. Fritz came out of the brush beside the trail and went running around the moose, barking and jumping.

"Fritz! No!" I yelled.

But Fritz didn't listen. He snapped at the back legs of the moose. Instead of fighting back, though, the moose just gave up. It ran back into the lake until most of its body had disappeared under the water.

Fritz came trotting down the old road looking pleased with himself.

"Fritz has been so protective of us. Even when we don't even need it!" I said. "I'm going to make sure Dad buys him a big steak when we get home!"

We started walking again. I was deep in thought about the area we were in and how far we had traveled these past days. All of a sudden Josh broke into my thoughts.

"Tim, is that an apple tree over there?" he asked in an excited voice.

I couldn't believe my eyes. The apples were small. But they were a welcome change from berries!

"I don't believe it!" I exclaimed.

I ran over to the apple tree. Josh followed as fast as his sore ankle would let him.

The birds had spoiled many of the apples. But more than we could eat or carry were edible.

We both ate too many apples. And we decided that these apples tasted better than any ice-cream sundae we had ever eaten. We filled our pockets and the backpack.

We traveled another mile or so and set up camp beside a lake. We were both so full of apples we couldn't think of eating anything else.

Dusk came sneaking up on us, erasing the bright sunlight of the day. And shadows once again made the forest a foreign place. The animals rule here, I thought. We're unwelcome visitors.

To seem to prove that point, a pack of wolves erupted into their evening howl. They were much closer tonight.

We have to keep the fire burning bright tonight, I thought.

"Josh if you wake up and the fire is low, be sure to wake me. Those wolves make my spine tingle," I said.

Every time I put wood on the fire, I could hear the howling of wolves. They must be talking to one another, I thought. And it's probably about us.

Fritz growled several times during the night. The funny feeling that something was out there was with me each time I woke up.

The night was dark. And I had the pistol beside me while I tried to sleep off and on.

10

A ROUGH RIDE HOME

During the night I awoke to what I thought was another wolf howling. But it was different from the other wolf sounds. More high-pitched. It gradually dawned on me what it was.

Had I been dreaming? I waited until morning to tell Josh the news.

I crawled out from under the tarp, put wood on the coals, and went to shake Josh.

"Josh! Josh!" I cried. "I can't believe it. I think I heard a train whistle during the night!"

Josh practically jumped out from under the tarp. "It's about time!" he said. He was all smiles.

We must have been a sight as we danced around and around in the forest. Our clothes were dirty and torn. And we were holding on to each other's hands. Just like a couple of four-year-olds. And Fritz was barking and jumping at us. It seemed so long since we had felt like this!

We were soon on our way. Off to find the railroad tracks!

We had traveled quite a while. But as we were passing a small lake, we heard the train whistle. It was much closer than the one I had heard last night.

So it hadn't been a dream!

"That sounded close!" I told Josh. "I'll bet we're not much farther than three or four miles from the tracks!"

We started traveling in a northern direction. It was tougher traveling. But we wanted to find those tracks as soon as we could.

It was almost sundown when we saw the sun glaring off a bright object. Yes! Yes! There were the well-used tracks we were looking for!

Once again we threw everything on the ground and did a goofy dance!

I started to make a fire. "Do you realize this may be the last fire we have to make?" I asked Josh.

The night was cold. I could see my breath as I gathered wood and tinder for the fire.

We weren't sure when the next train would come by. We had heard one whistle today. Would the next one be tonight or tomorrow morning? I wondered.

I looked on the map. We had changed directions after we heard the train whistle. It was hard to tell exactly where we were.

It was a cold night. And in the morning the eastern horizon was showing a faint glint of light as I crawled out from under the tarp.

I got out my logbook. Would this be the last time I would report from the wilderness?

It's funny to think about how mad I used to feel at my brother over little things. Now I feel like I understand him a little better. I don't think I would've made it through this without him. No one had better ever say anything bad about

Josh to me. I've been protecting him in the wilderness. And it'll be my duty to protect him when we get back home.

We'll never be quite the same, I thought as I put down the pencil. We will never be the same spoiled kids. Like I now realized we had been before.

After I shook Josh awake, I looked around for Fritz. But he was nowhere in sight. I felt a sinking feeling in my stomach. I remembered the howling of the wolves I had heard the past few nights. I hoped nothing had happened to Fritz. Not when we were so close to being rescued.

I decided not to mention anything to Josh. I'd protect him from this for now.

I shook Josh again and said, "Maybe today will be the day we can call Mom and Dad!"

Josh began crawling out from under the tarp. This morning instead of waking up grumpy, he awoke with a smile.

"When do you think another train will pass by?" he asked.

"I don't know," I answered. "I hope it's soon! Let's get all of our stuff packed up so we're ready."

Josh started folding up the tarp. And I put my logbook and pencil in my backpack.

All of a sudden Josh stopped folding. "Have you seen Fritz?" he asked.

I was getting nervous. Usually Fritz came around when Josh got up. I didn't want to upset Josh. Not when things were finally looking up.

"Tim?" Josh asked. "Are you deaf?"

Just in time, Fritz appeared out of the brush. He was running and barking.

I let out my breath and smiled. I was so glad Fritz was okay. We'd come through too much to lose him now!

"There you are!" Josh yelled. We both bent down to pet him.

As we were petting him, I heard rustling in the brush and trees from where Fritz had come. I got nervous. It sounded like something big. Maybe more than one animal. Thoughts of the bear and moose went through my head.

I remembered from that wilderness show I had watched that they actually have lynx in Canada! But I wasn't going to let a bear, wolf, lynx, or whatever spoil our plans of being rescued!

I pulled my pistol from the holster. I had been wearing it so long, it felt like a part of me now.

"Go hide!" I yelled to Josh. "And take Fritz with you!"

Josh scooped up Fritz and ran the opposite direction.

I had my gun aimed at the area I figured the animals would come from. The rustling was getting closer. All of a sudden, the creatures burst out of the trees!

I had to blink to make sure I wasn't seeing things. There stood two men in hunting clothes!

One was a rather large man. He had a beard that covered most of his face and much of his neck. He wore a brown hunting outfit with a bright red shirt.

The other man was smaller and dressed in bright orange. His shaggy brown hair hung from the bottom of his orange cap. Both carried guns.

The hunters were so surprised that they stopped and stared for a few seconds. I stood with my mouth open and stared back. Then I remembered my pistol. I quickly lowered it and put it back in my holster.

From behind a bush, I heard Josh start to sob. Then he ran over and stood beside me.

Finally the hunters walked up to us. The one dressed in orange spoke first. "Where did you boys come from anyway?"

I understood their surprise. Who would expect to see two dirty boys and a dog out in the middle of nowhere? We told the men our sad story.

"The dog came up to us," the large hunter said. "We thought he was a lost hunting dog. But he acted strange. As if he wanted us to follow him.

We didn't have any idea he would lead us to anyone! You certainly have a smart dog!"

I had to smile when Josh asked, "Do you have anything to eat that doesn't taste like fish?"

Like magic, the hunters pulled pop, sandwiches, and potato chips out of the backpacks they were carrying. The sandwiches were delicious. And the pop tasted much better than lake water.

Instead of hunting, the men we now knew as Jim and Ted helped us pack up. We were soon sitting in the back of an old pickup the men called their hunting pickup. It was about one-half rust with green paint showing through.

The ride was rough. But who cared?

We soon would be able to call Mom and Dad! And then we'd be able to go home. Ely, Minnesota, had never sounded so good!

As we rode toward a town and a telephone, dust swirled from behind the pickup. It reminded me of the smoke that tangled itself into the sky from the many fires we had made.

After much bumping around in the back of the old pickup, I looked ahead. I saw a church steeple through the trees. Soon we were in the outskirts of a small town. Even smaller than Ely, I noticed.

An old sign hung crooked from a post. It was weathered from many years in the Canadian winters and summers. And it read, "Balkhurst City Limits."

"Look, Josh," I said. "This town doesn't even have paved streets."

Josh thought that was weird. Even Ely had paved streets.

In the center of town was a well-kept red building. In front of it, several horses were tethered on a hitching post. The sign on the front of the building read, "District Headquarters of the Royal Canadian Mounted Police."

The Mountie we talked to was a very nice man. He introduced himself as Jacob Weaver. I sadly pointed out on our map where Bob's body could be found.

"Before you do anything else, you kids need to call your parents," Mr. Weaver said. "We have several phones. And you can both talk at the same time. I'm sure this will be the most important phone call your parents will ever get."

I didn't know why, but I was kind of nervous to call. We had been through so much. And I wouldn't know where to begin explaining it all.

"I have four boys," Mr. Weaver continued. "I bet we have some extra clothes that will fit both of you. We'll have a place for you to sleep too."

Finally the Mountie dialed the long-distance number. And then he left to get some clothes that would fit us both.

Josh was on one phone, and I was on the other.

Ring . . . Ring . . . Ring . . . With each ring, my nervousness decreased. Finally we heard Mom's familiar voice say, "Hello."

I spoke into the phone first. "Mom, it's me!" I cried.

Josh practically screamed, "I'm here too!"

I heard Mom crying and calling for Dad.

"I've never been so glad to hear anyone's voices!" Mom sobbed. "Where are you? Are you okay? Are you hurt?"

I assured her and Dad, who had just picked up another phone, that we were fine. Then I broke the news about Bob. And that we were in a town named Balkhurst in Canada.

"We were so afraid you were killed in a plane crash. The police thought that the plane had disappeared into one of the lakes nearby," Dad said. There was a short, uncomfortable pause. Dad cleared his throat. Then his voice changed from sad to excited. "We'll be up to get you as fast as we can!"

Our world was once more going to be normal. Soon we would see our parents. Neither Josh nor I would ever take our parents for granted again. I was sure of that!

And I would see Rich. And Ann. I wasn't sure I would want to talk about everything right away.

But I was sure that when I did, they would want to hear every detail.

The next morning Mr. Weaver handed me a newspaper. The headline brought back many memories, many things I wasn't ready to remember. It read, "A Wilderness Adventure."

I was quite proud of the story, though. "I told the reporter as much as I could remember about your days in the wilderness," Mr. Weaver said.

The article started like this.

A WILDERNESS ADVENTURE

A 15-year-old boy from Ely, Minnesota, led his 12-year-old brother and the family dog out of the wilderness of Canada. The pilot of the unscheduled plane they were on had a fatal heart attack while landing on one of Canada's many lakes. Living on berries, fish, and apples, Tim Jeffries led the trio to safety during a 12-day ordeal. The trio traveled through many miles of uncharted wilderness.

There was more. But I couldn't read it right now. I had a lot to think about. I didn't think I was a hero. I did what I had to do to protect my brother. And he was a big help picking berries and keeping me company.

And what about Fritz? He did his part to keep us safe. I would never think of him as a mutt again.

And then there was Bob. In the middle of a heart attack, he managed to get my brother and me safely on the ground. If anyone was a hero, he was!

I clipped the article and put it in my logbook. I would read it later. After all my feelings were sorted out.

I wasn't sure how many miles it was from Ely to Balkhurst. But I hoped Mom and Dad would get here soon.

After all, I had to finish mowing the grass.